Tiara
Club

at Emerald
Castle

For Princess Brittany, Princess Georgie
and all their friends at Sculthorpe
Primary School

VF

With very special thanks to JD

www.tiaraclub.co.uk

ORCHARD BOOKS
338 Euston Road, London NW1 3BH
Orchard Books Australia
Level 17/207 Kent St, Sydney, NSW 2000

A Paperback Original
First published in 2008 by Orchard Books
Text © Vivian French 2008
Cover illustration © Sarah Gibb 2008
Inside illustrations © Orchard Books 2008

The right of Vivian French to be identified as the author of this
work has been asserted by her in accordance with the
Copyright, Designs and Patents Act, 1988.

A CIP catalogue record for this book is available
from the British Library.

ISBN 978 1 84616 869 7

1 3 5 7 9 10 8 6 4 2

Printed in Great Britain

Orchard Books is a division of Hachette Children's Books,
an Hachette Livre UK company.

www.hachettelivre.co.uk

The Tiara Club

at Emerald Castle

Princess Amelia

and the Silver Seal

By Vivian French

ORCHARD BOOKS

The Royal Palace Academy
for the Preparation of Perfect Princesses

(Known to our students as "*The Princess Academy*")

OUR SCHOOL MOTTO:
*A Perfect Princess always thinks of others
before herself, and is kind, caring and truthful.*

**Emerald Castle offers a complete education for
Tiara Club princesses while taking full advantage of
our seaside situation. The curriculum includes:**

A visit to Emerald Sea World Aquarium and Education Pool	*Swimming lessons (safely supervised at all times)*
A visit to Seabird Island	*Whale watching*

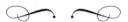

**Our headteacher, Queen Gwendoline, is present at all
times, and students are well looked after by the school
Fairy Godmother, Fairy Angora.**

Our resident staff and visiting experts include:

QUEEN MOLLY (Sports and games)	*KING JONATHAN (Captain of the Royal Yacht)*
LORD HENRY (Natural History)	*QUEEN MOTHER MATILDA (Etiquette, Posture and Flower Arranging)*

We award tiara points to encourage our Tiara Club princesses towards the next level. All princesses who win enough points at Emerald Castle will be presented with their Emerald Sashes and attend a celebration ball.

Emerald Sash Tiara Club princesses are invited to return to Diamond Turrets, our superb residence for Perfect Princesses, where they may continue their education at a higher level.

PLEASE NOTE:
Princesses are expected to arrive at the Academy with a *minimum* of:

TWENTY BALLGOWNS
(with all necessary hoops, petticoats, etc)

TWELVE DAY DRESSES

SEVEN GOWNS
suitable for garden parties, and other special day occasions

TWELVE TIARAS

DANCING SHOES
five pairs

VELVET SLIPPERS
three pairs

RIDING BOOTS
two pairs

Swimming costumes, playsuits, parasols, sun hats and other essential outdoor accessories as required

Oh, I'm SO excited! Are you?
I can't believe it's another new term
and we're here at Emerald Castle! And
you've come to join Daffodil Room with
the rest of us...that's BRILLIANT!
Leah, Ruby, Millie, Rachel and Zoe are
thrilled to bits. Whoops! I haven't told
you who I am. I'm Princess Amelia.
Welcome to Daffodil Room!

Chapter One

When my dad got a letter from Queen Mother Matilda, I nearly had a heart attack. I mean, it was the last day of the holidays, so WHY was she writing? She's one of our teachers at the Princess Academy, and I think she's a little bit scary.

I tried to remember if I'd done

anything dreadful the term before, but I couldn't...and then Dad called me up to his end of the table. (Do you have an absolutely VAST table in your castle? Ours is big enough for a party of at least a hundred kings and queens, and I used to slide on it when I was little.)

Dad coughed before he spoke. He always does that. Sometimes I think it's because he can't remember my name. He and Mum are just about ALWAYS away on some kind of tour or palace business. It's a good thing I've got six big brothers to keep me company!

"Ahem. Did you know Emerald Castle was by the sea, Amelia?" he asked.

I stared at him. What was he talking about?

"I thought not." My father shook his head in a My Daughter Is So Useless kind of way. "It seems you left Pearl Palace in such a rush at the end of last term you forgot your information pack. Fortunately for you someone found it lying on your bed in Daffodil Room, and now Queen Mother Matilda has sent it on. You really MUST try and be more careful in the future!"

"I'm very sorry," I said, and I tried to look as if I was, but my mind was whirling! By the sea? That sounded SO exciting.

My father handed me the letter and a list.

"You'd better check you've got everything you need," he said. "I don't suppose you've packed a parasol!" And he laughed, and went on eating his toast.

I asked if I could be excused, and absolutely flew up to my bedroom to study the list. I thought I'd finished my packing, but Dad was quite right. I hadn't packed ANYTHING suitable for the seaside! *Sun hats, playsuits, sand shoes, swimming costumes.* I had those in my cupboard – but I didn't have a parasol. I rushed off to find my mother.

"Darling!" she said. "Now, let me see..." She went to her dressing room, and came back with the sweetest little white lace parasol covered in sparkly beads.

"Oooh! It's so GORGEOUS!" I gave Mum a hug, and I sang loudly as I finished my packing. The seaside is just my most FAVOURITE place, and I was going to be there with all my best friends!

When the coach rolled round to the front door the following morning I was waiting on the front step. My brothers teased me and said I obviously hated

being at home, but they stood in
a row with Dad and waved as the
coach rolled away down the drive.

Mum was coming with me as far as Rachel's castle, and then Rachel and I were going to travel on to Emerald Castle on our own. Is it any wonder I was excited?

Chapter Two

When we first saw the sea, Rachel and I absolutely screamed, we were so thrilled. The water was the most gorgeous sparkly blue, and the sand really was golden. As we got closer we could see Emerald Castle perched on the cliffs above the bay, and a little winding path twisting down to the beach.

"WOW!" Rachel breathed as our carriage finally rolled in between the school gates. "Isn't this just the best ever?"

"FANTASTIC!" I agreed, and the coach had hardly stopped before we were tumbling out and rushing in through the huge front door in the most unprincessy way. Leah, Ruby, Millie and Zoe were in the main hall sorting out their luggage, but when they saw us they dropped everything and ran to give us a hug.

"Daffodil Room!" boomed a familiar voice, and there was Fairy G, our school fairy godmother.

"I know you're pleased to see each other and I'm delighted to see you, too, but you really MUST hurry up! Queen Gwendoline has ordered tea in the dining hall at four o'clock, and she does NOT like her students to be late."

"Sorry, Fairy G," we chorused, and Rachel and I went to organise getting our trunks from the coach. Then we followed our friends upstairs to Daffodil Room – and it was WONDERFUL!

"It's so much prettier than our room in Pearl Palace," Ruby said happily as she twirled in the middle of the floor.

"I know." Zoe patted her yellow satin bedspread. "It's gorgeous."

"Has anyone seen Diamonde and Gruella?" Millie asked as she brushed her hair. "Do you think they'll be as awful as they were last term?"

"I heard Diamonde talking to Fairy G," Leah giggled. "She was complaining because she and Gruella have been given a room in the tower, and she thinks there are too many stairs."

"Sounds much the same as usual," I said, and then I saw the time. "Ooops! We'd better go!"

We weren't quite the last students to reach the dining hall, but our new head teacher was frowning as we hurried in. She was quite young, but she looked very stern, and I began to feel a bit nervous – especially when she looked at a piece of paper in her hand and called, "Princess Amelia! Come here, please!"

I scurried across, and made a deep curtsey.

"Good afternoon, Your Majesty."

"Queen Mother Matilda tells me she had to send you your Emerald Castle Information Pack. Apparently you left it in your room in Pearl Palace. Is that correct, Princess Amelia?"

"I'm so sorry, Your Majesty," I quavered. "It was very silly of me."

"It was." Queen Gwendoline gave me a horribly cold look. "I shall expect you to try harder this term. I do not approve of carelessness. Do you understand?"

"I understand, Your Majesty," I whispered.

"Good. Now, go back to your table, and remember! I will be watching you, Princess Amelia!"

I went back to my friends feeling absolutely terrible – and it didn't help when Diamonde and Gruella sniggered as I walked past them.

I sat down next to Rachel, but I couldn't eat a thing. I'd been SO looking forward to being at Emerald Castle – and now it was all going wrong!

Chapter Three

I didn't sleep very well that night,
even though we had such a lovely
room. I kept dreaming I'd lost my
books, or my tiara, and Queen
Gwendoline was telling me off.
When the first bell rang I was
already awake and dressed, and
my friends looked at me in
surprise as they sat up in bed.

"Are you OK, Amelia?" Millie asked. I shrugged.

"Sort of. I'm just a bit worried about Queen Gwendoline."

Ruby nodded. "My cousin was here a couple of years ago, and she told me she was terrified for the first week, and then she found out Queen Gwen was actually really kind."

"H'm," I said. "I do hope she's right! Does anyone know what we're doing today?"

"We've got a swimming lesson straight after breakfast." Zoe didn't sound terribly enthusiastic. "Queen Molly's going to meet us at the beach." She sighed. "I hate swimming lessons – I just KNOW I'm never going to learn to swim!"

Millie leant over and gave Zoe a hug. "It's easier swimming in the sea – honestly! And we'll help you."

"You'll have to help me too," Leah said cheerfully. "I ALWAYS sink! And sea water tastes SO disgusting."

Zoe laughed, and we finished getting dressed and hurried downstairs. Luckily Fairy G and Fairy Angora (her assistant) were in charge of breakfast, so we didn't see Queen Gwendoline.

Queen Molly came bustling in just as we were clearing away the plates.

"Good morning, princesses!" she said. "We're going to have SUCH a fabulous morning. Please meet me on the beach in half an hour, and don't forget to use your parasols as you walk down the path. We don't want any burnt noses!"

We fetched our swimming costumes and towels, then headed for the beach. My friends loved my pretty parasol, but Diamonde made a face as she hurried past with Gruella.

"Oooh! How VERY fancy!" she sneered, but before I could answer she pulled Gruella into the nearest changing hut, and slammed the door. Leah, Ruby and I waited for Millie, Rachel and Zoe, and then walked on to the huts further down the beach. By the time we were changed Queen Molly was marching up and down the sand, and she ordered us to run into the sea.

"No deeper than your waists, princesses!" she called. "And anyone who can't swim must wear arm bands!"

Millie, Ruby, Rachel and

I plunged into the turquoise blue water, while Leah and Zoe collected their bands. The sea felt quite warm once you got used to it, and we splashed about happily until Queen Molly was ready.

"We'll begin with the breast stroke," she said. "Let me see you swim to that large rock and back, but please DON'T go round it. You wouldn't be out of your depth; the water is very shallow here, but I want to be able to see you at all times. Non-swimmers, you stay with me."

I don't want to sound boastful, but I'm quite a fast swimmer, and

so is Rachel. She and I were soon
in front of all the others, and we
reached the rock way ahead of
everyone else. I was about to turn
to go back when I heard a strange
noise; it sounded a little bit like
a kitten mewing.

"Can you hear that?" I asked, and Rachel nodded.

"Maybe we'd better go and have a look," I said. "Whatever it is sounds SO sad."

"But what about Queen Molly saying we shouldn't go behind the rock?" Rachel asked anxiously. I dithered, but then the noise came again.

"We'll be very quick," I said.

Chapter Four

It was a good thing the water
wasn't very deep, or I might have
sunk with surprise as we swam
round the rock. There, crouched
on a little ledge facing out to
sea, was the SWEETEST little
silver seal. At first I thought he
was just having a rest, but when
I looked closer I saw he was

tangled in a mess of old rope and wire.

"Rachel!" I whispered. "Look!"

Rachel came to stand beside me, and the poor seal gave an agonised grunt, and tried to wriggle free, but he was caught fast.

"It's all right," I soothed, "we won't hurt you..." I put out my hand and gently stroked his head. Then, as carefully as I could, I began to unknot the bits of rope and wire. The silver seal stared at me with his huge black eyes, and I'm sure he knew I was trying to help him because he didn't struggle at all. Rachel took the bits of wire and rope as I handed them to her, and although it seemed to take ages and ages it could only have been a few seconds before the little seal was free. He lifted up his head and made a strange coughing kind of noise, and there was an answering bark.

Rachel and I jumped as a huge fully grown seal came swirling round the rock towards us. The silver seal squeaked ecstatically and flopped into the water, and his mother nuzzled him before they both swam away.

As we watched them go Diamonde and Gruella splashed round the corner of the rock from the other side. They followed our gaze, and Gruella went pale.

"Are those sharks?" she gasped.

"No, it's a baby seal and his mother," Rachel said. "The baby was stuck on a ledge, and Amelia set him free. Look!" She showed Gruella the bits of rope and wire. "He was caught up in these!"

Diamonde sniffed. "Queen Molly wants to know why you've been here so long, and Queen Gwendoline's arrived and she's looking furious."

At once my stomach felt as if it was full of whirling butterflies, but Rachel gave me a reassuring smile. "Don't worry," she said. "You were being a Perfect Princess and doing a Good Deed."

Diamonde's eyes suddenly brightened, and she turned back towards us. "That's right," she said, and snatched the rope and wire from Rachel's hands. "Here – I'll carry these for you.

Let's go, Gruella." And before Rachel or I could say a word the twins were half walking, half swimming round the rock and out of sight.

"Why did she do that do you think?" I wondered.

"We'll soon find out," Rachel said. "Come on. You look really shivery!"

I nodded. Rachel was right; I was so cold I could only swim really slowly. As we came in sight of the shore we saw Diamonde and Gruella talking to Queen Gwendoline and Queen Molly. They were pointing back towards the rock, and our friends were crowding round as if the twins were telling an amazing story.

By the time we were close enough
to hear what they were saying
Queen Gwendoline was looking
delighted, and Queen Molly
was beaming.

"So the little seal kissed us on our
noses to say thank you to us – "
Diamonde went on talking as we

walked up the sandy beach towards her – "and then he swam to his mother, and his mother bowed to us, and the two of them swam away together!"

"Well DONE, girls!" Queen Molly clapped her hands, and all our classmates clapped as well.

Gruella suddenly noticed us, and she gave a little squeal. "Oh, look! Here are Amelia and Rachel! They didn't help the baby seal at all, did they, Diamonde?" Diamonde gave us a snooty look.

"How could they? They were MUCH too busy hiding behind the rock and messing about.'"

Queen Gwendoline folded her arms and gave me and Rachel the chilliest stare.

"Get yourselves dry and dressed, please," she told us, "and then come and find me in my study!" And she swept away.

Chapter Five

By the time Rachel and I were standing outside Queen Gwendoline's door my knees were shaking. Rachel was much braver than me; she walked straight in, but I noticed she did wobble a little bit as she curtsied. Queen Gwendoline was sitting behind her desk; I could hardly look at her, because I was so sure she was going to be absolutely furious with us – but then I saw lovely Fairy G standing by the window, and I felt a million times better.

"Princess Amelia and Princess Rachel," Queen Gwendoline said slowly, "I must tell you that you are fortunate in having a good friend in Fairy G. I was very angry when I heard from Queen Molly that you had disobeyed her instructions, but Fairy G promises you must have had a reason. Could you tell me what that reason was?"

I took a deep breath, and hoped my voice wouldn't squeak.

"If you please, Your Majesty, I heard the baby seal crying, although we didn't know it was a seal, of course. And we thought we'd better go and look."

"I see." Queen Gwendoline nodded. "So what happened then?"

I didn't answer her at once. What could I say? Diamonde had told our head teacher she and Gruella had rescued the seal, and I couldn't be a horrible telltale and say she'd been telling lies. I hesitated, but Rachel stepped forward.

"We found the silver seal all tangled up, and Amelia spent ages setting him free," she said.

Queen Gwendoline frowned. "But Diamonde and Gruella showed me the rope and wire he was tangled in. And you must have heard them telling me how they released him, and he swam off with his mother. Indeed, I saw the two seals myself. Both are regular visitors to this shore, and I know them well. If Amelia saved the silver seal, why didn't you speak out straight away?"

Rachel and I looked at each other.

How could we have interrupted when the twins were telling their story? Nobody there would have believed us – but we couldn't say that to our head teacher. The silence seemed to go on and on...until Fairy G suddenly laughed. "Your Majesty," she said, "Come and look out of the window!"

Queen Gwendoline got up and strode to the window, and Rachel and I followed her – and our eyes opened wide. There, on the rocks below, was a large shining seal, and she was clapping her flippers and looking up at Emerald Castle.

And as Fairy G opened the window we could hear her calling – a weird noise in between a bark and a cough.

"I'd say she wants to thank her baby's rescuers," Fairy G said, and she gave me the teeniest wink. "I think it would be MOST interesting if we asked all our princesses to come down to the beach and meet her."

Chapter Six

Millie told me later that Queen Mother Matilda was most annoyed that her lesson on How to Step Safely and Gracefully Into a Rocking Boat had been cancelled, but there was nothing she could do. Queen Gwendoline led the procession down to the beach, and Diamonde and

Gruella walked beside her. Fairy G followed at the very end, with me and Rachel. As we got nearer and nearer we could see the seal looking more and more excited.

"Please stop now," Queen Gwendoline said as we reached the sand. "Stay where you are, and we'll see what Oceana does."

"Is that the seal's name?" I whispered to Fairy G, and she nodded.

We stood in our long line, our parasols protecting us from the sun, and waited. Oceana put her head on one side, and slithered off the rock – and we suddenly saw the little silver seal behind her.

Slowly they made their way towards us, and I could see Diamonde begin to fidget as Oceana passed her by without a second glance. Queen Gwendoline raised her eyebrows, but she said nothing.

On and on Oceana waddled, while her baby flipped and flopped beside her. It wasn't until they finally reached Rachel and me that he began to bounce on his flippers and tail, and hurried forward until he was almost on top of my feet.

He looked up at me, and his eyes were SO big and black – and I was almost certain that he smiled. Oceana was right behind him, and when she reached Rachel and me she lifted up a flipper – and pointed at us.

I curtsied. It may sound a silly thing to do, but she looked really queenly, and even though she had to waddle on the sand there was something wonderfully graceful about the way she dropped her head, then looked us in the eyes.

"Well done, Oceana," Fairy G said quietly as Queen Gwendoline

came sweeping down the beach towards us.

"Princess Amelia and Princess Rachel! It seems it was INDEED you who saved the silver seal.

I must apologise for not having investigated more thoroughly before accusing you." She stroked Oceana's head, and the big seal turned so our head teacher could scratch her neck. "Oceana always remembers people who have helped her, and her baby is very precious to her."

"He's adorable," I said, and I bent down to tickle him under his chin.

"I'm sure you'll see him again." Queen Gwendoline smiled, and I found myself thinking, "Oh! She IS nice! She looks QUITE different now!"

"Now, I must speak to the twins.
I shall take them back to Emerald
Castle, and then I shall send out
the cooks and the pages with
a special picnic lunch. I'd say
these princesses deserved a treat,
wouldn't you, Fairy G?"

Fairy G chuckled. "I certainly would. And maybe I can make them all more comfortable..." and she waved her wand round

and round. A flurry of stars flew up in the air, and when they landed on the sandy beach they burst into the prettiest rugs and cushions.

Oceana gave a little grunt of surprise, and she and her baby slipped back into the water... but a moment later we saw them settling happily back on their rock.

Diamonde and Gruella didn't look at me as they trailed back to Emerald Castle, and we didn't see them again that day... but the rest of us had SUCH a gorgeous time! We had the most delicious lunch on the beach.

Afterwards Fairy G said we could all explore...and we found the sweetest little rock pools and quiet sandy coves, and even a couple of caves hung with pretty seaweed!

When we were getting ready for bed that evening, I felt so happy I almost burst. The sea was right outside my bedroom window, and I had six perfect friends to share it all with. Leah, Ruby, Millie, Rachel, Zoe...

And you!

Don't miss  website at:

www.tiaraclub.co.uk

Keep up to date with the latest
Tiara Club books and meet all
your favourite princesses!

There is SO much to see and do,
including games and activities. You can
even become an exclusive member of the
Tiara Club Princess Academy.

PLUS, there's an exciting
Emerald Castle competition
with a truly AMAZING prize!

Be a Perfect Princess – check it out today!

What happens next?
Find out in

Princess Leah
and the Golden Seahorse

Hello – and do you like the seaside?
I absolutely LOVE it – which is why I'm
VERY happy Emerald Castle is by the sea.
I'm so lucky to be here – especially as
you've come to keep me company. And
Amelia, Ruby, Millie, Rachel and Zoe are
here too – we're the Daffodil Room
princesses. Oh! Did I tell you who I am?
I'm Princess Leah! How do you do?

When we first got to Emerald Castle I thought our headteacher, Queen Gwendoline, was horribly fierce, but luckily I was wrong. She can be stern, but it's only because she wants us to be totally PERFECT princesses. Most of the time she's very smiley, and she thinks up a new project for us practically every single day. We weren't at all surprised when she came marching in while we were eating our breakfast to tell us about yet another idea.

"Good morning, princesses!" she said cheerfully. "I've got SUCH a lovely outing planned for you!

Fairy Angora is going to take you to Emerald Sea World. It's a wonderful place; you'll walk down and down a long dark passage until you're actually UNDERNEATH Emerald Bay, and then you'll come to a room with a glass ceiling – and you'll see all kinds of beautiful fish swimming above you!"

The horrible twins, Diamonde and Gruella, were sitting at the table next to ours, and I heard Diamonde whisper, "BORING!"

Luckily our headteacher didn't hear her, and she went on, "There's an aquarium as well, with an education pool that has a wonderful golden seahorse in it – one of the very few golden seahorses in the world! Of course," and for a second Queen Gwendoline looked ferocious, "you will NOT touch the seahorse." She smiled again. "And I have another surprise. A group from the Princes' Academy have been studying marine life, and they've very kindly agreed to show you the creatures in the education pool. I want to thank them, so I thought we might end the day with a party here at Emerald Castle."

~ *Want to read more?* ~
Princess Leah and the Golden Seahorse
is out now!

This summer, look out for

Emerald Ball

Vivian French

ISBN: 978 1 84616 881 9

Two stories in one fabulous book!